Learning To Drive...

Here I am in traffic court

**Happy Driving Lesson
Pulled Over by the Cops
Bad Day at Traffic Court
I Go Before the Judge**

**By Anne Wilensky
Cartoons by Bill Pyne (aka Billy Stampone)**

Published by Haiku Helen Press

Published May 2013
© 2013 by Anne Pyne

Written, edited, and published by Anne Pyne

Cartoons on front cover and inside book by Bill Pyne aka Billy Stampone

ISBN 978-0-9840976-4-7

Contact information: Willard Kraft
(520) 465-0999
5152 East 8th Street, Tucson, AZ 85711

First edition
Printed in the United States of America.

The day before Christmas 2012

Yesterday I went back to my driving

Jim doesn't have an easy time putting up with Anne

Yesterday I went back to my driving. I haven't driven since the rains came. I no longer remember when that was. It feels like a world ago.

I hadn't driven in so long that when Jim suggested it yesterday I knew if I didn't do it now I would never do it again.

I had lost all connection to driving. The last two times I had done it had not been a good experience.

It had been far too tense for me driving in town. Driving in traffic with other cars on the road. It had not been pleasurable at all. I hadn't wanted to do it again.

It just seemed so much simpler to let Jim drive me everywhere, sit back and relax.

Yesterday was cold but bright sun was shining. It was Sunday. I really did feel like *now or never*.

"OK" I said. "Let's go to the country then. You can wash the windshield for me when we stop on the way for gas."

I was quiet all the way. I have no grip on my mood at all now. I have no idea what makes me want to laugh and play and kid around with him in the car. Like the day before when he had driven me for my errands.

Or why I was so quiet yesterday. Why I just wanted to sit quietly and say nothing. Look out the window. Just be quiet.

We stopped for gas, he washed the windshield. I went inside and bought two peanut butter on crackers.

He drove me to Corona Road. Without any fanfare at all

we changed seats and I simply began driving.

I drove slowly the whole time. He went out of his mind the whole time. All the way up Corona Road, all the way down Los Reales, all the way to the end of Swan Road I drove slowly. I had it in 4th but never went above 20 miles an hour.

He went out of his mind the whole time. He insisted every which way to Sunday that I step on it.

I was the only car on the road the whole time. I figured I wasn't bothering anyone.

He carried on that I was going 20 miles an hour. "I put up with it when you do this in your own neighborhood," he kept saying. "I don't want to put up with it now," he kept saying.

"Tough" I said. "Turn on the radio" I said, "you can listen to the radio."

The truck has no radio. This is a joke I make to amuse myself.

"The speed limit here is 55 you have to go the speed limit," he said.

"You can read the article about the Mass Awakening by Archangel Raphael while I'm driving.

"You can read it aloud to me" I said.

"I won't read it," he said. "Archangel Raphael is a nut."

"Turn on the radio then and listen to the game."

"There is no radio" he said.

"Now you are going 15 miles an hour!" he said.

"You're lucky you're going for a nice drive in the country on Sunday morning. Not every friend would do that for you. You are lucky to have a wonderful friend like me."

No man was more miserable as he was driven that long forever stretch of Swan Road with not another car on the road by me at 20 miles an hour.

"This is torture," he kept saying.

I didn't care. I knew the best thing for me in whole world now was to be relaxed behind the wheel again. There had been a long time of me driving where I hadn't been relaxed at all. And it had taken its toll. I hadn't wanted to get behind the wheel again as a result.

I didn't mind all his complaining. It amused me. It gave conversation in the car while I was driving. It diverted me.

"Awww the open road" I said with enthusiasm.

"This is not the open road!" he said, "the open road is not driving 15 miles an hour."

I chuckled to myself.

"I love the open road" I said.

When we reached the end of Swan Road I did 6 tushy turns right in a row. That is what Jim and I call the 3 point turn which I have to do successfully on the Road Test to get my license.

They got to be called tushy turns because Jim kept saying "you turn the wheel in the direction you want your tushy to go," meaning the back of the truck.

Oddly enuf it relaxed Jim when I did 6 of them all in a row, and all of them perfectly. He had really wondered if my driving had regressed in long month of not doing it.

He thought maybe I really had gone back to square one. But I was so relaxed at driving such a long distance at only 20 miles an hour, it made me relaxed while I was doing my tushy turns. So I was able to do them fine.

I am beginning to see the whole key for driving for me is being relaxed behind the wheel.

On the way back to Los Reales Road I drove the same way but this time Jim did not complain. He was overjoyed by my tushy turns.

"I am not seeing any animals," I said.

"There aren't any animals," he said.

"I wonder why?" I said. "There aren't any birds in the

sky," I said looking up at the huge sky.

I said "We may as well get my cartons of cigarettes at the rez while we are all the way out here.

"You give me the directions till we get to Nogales Highway then we will change seats."

"You can drive on Nogales Highway" he said.

I ignored him.

I followed his directions till we came to a long stretch of road I hadn't been on before. There were cars on it but not that many. It was Sunday. It was fun for me to be on a road I had never been on before. With different view on the sides and a different view ahead of me.

By now I was relaxed and warmed up. I drove like a normal driver. I don't know why, it just seemed to come naturally to me. It felt natural going at a faster speed. Cars passed me who wanted to go faster. Fine with me. But I knew I was going a natural speed now. And it was fine.

Then I pulled expertly into the embankment right before Nogales Highway and let Jim take the wheel.

After we bought a whole box of cartons of cigarettes. And after Jim stopped at Nico's along the way home so I could get take-out Mexican food to eat when I got home, we got to my driveway.

"I'm not going to swim today," I said. "You did enuf. You helped me a lot. Just bring the cigarettes into the house for me then you are a free man all day."

Before we reached my house, a few miles up, he said "you drove spectacular."

I couldn't believe my ears. "Say it again," I said. "Say it again."

He said "Not in the beginning. In the beginning you were a black hole You got an F. But at the end you drove spectacular."

"Really?" I said. "Really? Say it again" I said.

Anne loves her driving lesson

Email on February 7 2013

Being stopped by the cops is no fun

I still do not have my drivers license, I have not yet taken my second road test. I had a big bump in the road 3 days ago because a girl cop pulled me over for driving in the bike lane.

I know that it is a no-no, but I was trying to go to the mini post office in my neighborhood. And when I wanted to make the left turn to it, I saw so many cars bearing down behind me, I just pulled into the bike lane so I would be out of everyone's way while I decided what to do.

Turned out there was cop car behind me and she had me pull into a driveway.

I had to sit there a whole hour. She discovered my learners permit had expired. Two times I got out of the truck to go over to her to find out what the problem is. I was starting to feel like I had committed a major crime.

She ordered me back in my vehicle. When I tried to ask her a question, she said "Do you have a comprehension problem?"

I said "no."

She said, "You were told to stay in your vehicle."

Then she said "Have you been drinking this morning?"

I said "I am insulted, I have never had a drink in my life but I want a cigarette."

She said "Get back in your vehicle!"

Jim my friend who is teaching me to drive was scared because they took his license too and he thought they would give him tickets for everything I did because he is my licensed driver.

Also they said they were deciding if my truck had to be

towed home.

Which makes no sense, Jim is there and can drive it home.

Finally the man cop came out to give me the two tickets. For driving in the bike lane and for expired license.

He asked me how long I have been learning how to drive, and was kind and understanding. She had been so hard assed with me and said "You are not allowed to drive barefoot."

I still don't know why it took her a whole hour, she must have been looking up all my violations.

It really shook me up and it shook Jim up too.

Love Annie

P.S. Ruthie looked it up on internet. It is *not* against the law to drive barefoot.

I go to court on February 28th.

Jim takes Anne swimming after the cops drive off. LOL she is stunned from her experience.

February 28th afternoon

I went to court this morning

Anne shows up at court

The cop had said to me I am giving you two tickets. One for driving in the bike lane and the other for expired license.

And he handed me the paper with the two citations on it

and little booklet with it.

Last week when I was very early after my swim at Y waiting for Jim to get me and it was too cold to wait outside, I sat in the waiting room and got out the citations and the booklet.

The booklet had some of the citations on it. For expired license it said $70 but if you go down and get another license and show that to the judge you don't have to pay it.

And since I had taken the written test the day after the tickets and gotten my new learners permit I saw I wouldn't have to pay that one.

But the other one driving in bike lane, the citation number with it wasn't on the booklet. So I had no idea how much that ticket would be.

At the bottom of the citation it said to go to court on February 28th, and court opens at 8 AM and it gave the address.

So yesterday I said to Jim, "Pick me up at 7:30 so I can be there at 8 AM when it opens.

"I'll probably finish at 10 AM so you can pick me up then and we can both go swimming."

I woke up at 6 AM this morning and even tho I wanted to go back to sleep I realized I have to get ready for court.

Yesterday I had painted my fingernails to look pretty for the judge. And of course all day I kept saying to myself what I will say to the judge.

So I forced myself to get up at 6 am, fed the kitties, put up my coffee, and organized for court.

I had my checkbook and my credit card so I could pay whatever it comes to. Plus I found 2 dollar bills, I put that in my change purse, along with two 20 dollar bills.

I changed my outfit a few times, I wanted to look nice but I didn't want to wear a bra.

And I got out the new pretty sandals I had bought at Payless last week.

At 6:30 I called Jim and woke him up. "Can you be here at 7:30?"

"Yes" he said.

I only got to have few sips of my coffee.

I reorganized my pocketbook so I would be sure to have all the paperwork for court. I had one minute before Jim drove into my driveway so I rushed out to paint my toenails.

And I put my swim bag, towel, and bathing suit in truck too for after court.

"When we go to court" I said, "you don't have to come

in with me, I am not afraid to talk to the judge.

"Why don't you go to your club and have wonderful jacuzzi, steam, and sauna and schmooze with your friends.

"Come back for me at 10 o'clock or 10:15, I am sure I will be finished then."

Going in thru the metal detector was so much fun, and I was laughing with the girl security guard in charge.

And she pointed to the courtroom for traffic tickets.

The line was so tiny because I was so early. So I asked the man ahead of me if he could hold my place so I could go to the ladies room.

He said "of course." But just then they opened the door, and he even let me ahead of him. What a gentleman!

The lady said "Go to window 5."

I was so surprised because I expected to walk into a court room.

I couldn't figure it out. Are the judges behind the windows and I tell them the story?

But at Window 5 was a very nice girl. I showed her my citation. She looked them both up on her computer.

She said "You can pay it all now or go to defensive driving school or see a judge."

I said "how much is the driving in bike lane one?"

She looked on her computer and said "199."

Plus I have to see the judge to show him I got my learners permit again and take away that fine.

So I said "I want to see the judge."

So she said "Fill out this paper. And you will get something in the mail in two weeks giving you an appointment to see the judge in a month."

"I didn't know that, no one told me that. I thought I would see the judge today. It is only ten after 8 and my friend won't come to pick me up till 10 o'clock. I don't have cell phone. Where can I call him?"

Her cell phone was right by her on her desk, along with her half eaten bagel. I hoped she would offer to call Jim.

But instead she said "I will show you where the pay phones are, meet me at the end of this."

She was very nice and took me down the hall and pointed out ladies room for me and public phones.

Luckily I saw I had a few quarters in my change purse. I didn't know where to call Jim. On his cell phone or call him at Racquet Club?

I decided to do his cell phone first in case he went home and not to Club.

I put in my quarter but it kept asking for 25 cents.

So I hung up and tried again.

And same thing happened

So I thought I don't know how to operate this public telephone

I went into an office and told the girl behind the desk the whole story. Her cell phone was sitting right there, I hoped she would offer. When she didn't I said "how do the public phones work?"

She said "I have no idea."

I was standing there totally flummoxed, I did not know what to do.

A cop came in and immediately began chatting with her. He was so enthusiastic to be there and chat with her.

And he was showing her pictures and games on his cell phone.

So I told him my story that I need help with the public telephone.

At some point I must have been near tears from all my frustration and desperation so my voice got louder with emotion.

He immediately ordered me "DON'T YELL AT ME!"

I probably hit bottom then.

I knew he was not going to help me. Instead he jeered at

me when I said "I put in my quarter."

He said "pay phones have not been a quarter for 20 years."

"How much are they now?" I asked

"I don't know" he said, "35 cents."

And then he taunted me. Making fun of my New York City accent. Imitating it.

Then he went back to showing her all the things on his cell phone. He was so happy talking to her.

I saw 3 telephone books on a shelf on the side and hoped I could find the phone number for Racquet Club. I was so glad when I found it. And folded the phone book to that page to take to the public phone.

"Where are you going with that phone book!" he barked at me.

"I am just taking it to public phone. I will bring it back. I am not stealing it."

Everything was crazy at the public phone. It said put in 4 quarters for 4 minutes.

So I put in 4 quarters and dialed Racquet Club. The book must have been out of date. Instead what I got was a recording asking "What is your emergency? Are you dying? Are you having a heart attack?"

I hung up and hoped my money would be returned. It was not.

Then I saw it said 50 cents for local call. I had two quarters left. I called Jim's cell phone.

When it rang 5 times I knew he is not at home but at the Club and since he never picks up his messages I hung up before the recording began "leave a message," hoping my quarters would be returned. They were not.

I brought the phonebook back and the policeman was still showing her everything on his cell phone. Calling out the names of cities, "San Antonio" and "San Diego" etc.

So I decided to go outside and have a cigarette.

I could not find any place to sit down and kept crossing streets. Finally I saw a place with a lot of benches. And went there.

It turned out to be the bus terminal. "Fine" I thought, "I will take the bus home."

It was about twenty to nine now. They had clock showing the time. When a bus pulled up I asked the driver "which is the bus to Swan and 5th?

He said "behind me."

I walked up and down looking at all the buses and the ones pulling in, but none of them were the right bus for me, they were all going someplace else.

When a bus pulled in and opened the door I saw "exact change needed."

I said "how much does it cost?"

He said "1.50."

I said "I have two dollars."

I had checked my change purse. He said "that is fine."

Finally I sat down on a bench, altho it was so cold in the shade. The bench in the sunshine was all filled up.

I saw a teenager with his cell phone. I debated for a while and then summoned up my courage. I had 20 cents left. I said I can give it to him if I can call my friend and say pick me up.

He said "I have no minutes left."

I could tell he thought I was a panhandler and was trying to get rid of me.

But then a nice miracle happened. A girl who was also standing there said she is also waiting for the Number 3 bus. And it is supposed to be arriving now and she doesn't know where it is.

She said "I am just going to take it to the other side of the tunnel. I could walk there but it is so cold in the tunnel."

You have to go thru a tunnel to get into or leave downtown.

She said "The bus is supposed to be here now. And my class is at 9 o'clock."

The clock said 5 to nine.

I said "I sure hope it comes so you are not late for class."

She said "It is OK my boyfriend knows I am late."

She said "That is our bus now but it has to pull around."

She sure knew her way around the buses.

And when it pulled around she got on right away. I said to the driver "I have two singles." And he pointed to the thing to put them both in. And they slid thru nicely.

I was so happy to be on the bus. I forgot I love buses and haven't been on one for almost 20 years. My first year in Tucson I took it twice when Bill did not want to drive me to the mall.

The back of the bus was elevated, you step up two steps. Of course I wanted to sit up high.

So I went to the last seat in last row in back of bus and sat by the window so I could look out.

And after the tunnel at the first stop I looked out the window and there was my friend from the bus terminal.

I knocked on the window with my rings. She looked up

and saw me and waved to me and I waved to her. I couldn't understand what school she went to, I didn't see any school.

But the friendliness made me happy.

I actually was completely happy during my bus ride. It was fun he went so slowly so I could look around. Jim drives so fast and is mainly mad at other drivers who hold him up.

Then I noticed the teenage boy sitting on the side seat. He had his magic markers out and was doing a tattoo on his hand. I found that so interesting to watch.

Then he got out his cell phone and used it as a mirror and combed his long hair and made it into a hair-do he liked. His hair was chin length. He shook it so it fell the way he liked. And studied it in his cell phone mirror.

I watched him for a long time, it was so interesting how he was making himself beautiful. Plus I loved looking out the window too.

Then a beautiful girl got on and that was so exciting. She was blond with glasses but her glasses made her even more beautiful. And I noticed she had black fishnet stockings and boots. She looked so alive. She was a joy to look at.

She had enormous purse. And first she took out the

tablet and did a few things with it. She used it as a mirror too. She pursed her lips and looked at herself.

Then she went into her enormous pocketbook and pulled out a paperback book. It was big, as big as my books. And I was so gratified to see someone still does read books.

Then my Higher Self said "Look away! You can't keep looking at her, it is called staring and it is rude."

So I forced my eyes off her and looked out the window again. I guess it was OK with the teenage boy because he was unaware of me, he was in his own world. He had now taken out two notebooks, but they had writing on cover.

I didn't know what it was about.

So I looked out the window all the way till we reached Columbus Road which is the road before mine, mine is Swan.

At first I couldn't figure out how you let the driver know you want him to stop. I know how you do it in NYC, you just pull the thing. But I didn't see the thing to pull and thought "maybe you press a button" but I didn't see a button.

But then I saw the thing to pull on other side of the bus, so looked up and there was one on my side too. Low down.

So after Columbus I pulled it. But to my surprise he made a stop in between before he got to my street. He thought that was what I wanted.

So I walked up to the front of the bus and said "I'm so sorry. I made a mistake. I'm going to Swan."

There was another bus driver standing next to him schmoozing the whole time.

When I said "I'm going to Swan" he said are you going to Condac?"

"Why" I said and burst out laughing, "do I look like a mental patient!"

I was laughing at my joke, I found it so funny.

My dog always used to take me to the Condac parking lot. It is near my house. She would go up to everybody and kiss them. Some of the people looked like they had not cracked a smile in 20 years. But they were happy when my dog gave them love. That's how I knew it was some kind of therapy center.

The parking lot is always full so I realize they have to show up once a month to renew their prescription.

Just when I was going to get off the bus a girl in front said to the driver she just wants to get off for a second to throw her tissue out.

"Hand it to me" I said, "I will put it in garbage can for you."

She gave me her tissue and I was still laughing at my joke and happy to do a favor.

So I hopped out in such a good mood and threw the tissue in the garbage can right next to bench at bus stop.

I went home as fast as I could and rushed in the house so I could call Jim before he left to pick me up at court.

I tried his cell phone twice, no answer. But I figured he would realize I was home when my name showed up.

Then I looked up Racquet Club on my computer. I asked the guy at the desk if Jim is there. And the guy said yes.

I said "Tell him Annie is home. Don't go to court. The judge would not see her."

He said he will give Jim the message.

Then I changed into my play clothes so I could rush outside with my comforter and lay in the sunshine.

I also heated up the coffee I never got to drink in the morning.

Jim called. "I'm home" I said. "I took the bus. They wouldn't let me see the judge.

"Come to my house, we will decide about swimming then."

I rushed off the phone because I really wanted to get to that glorious sunshine and lie down and drink my coffee.

I was surprised it took Jim so long to arrive. I thought "well maybe he is doing errands."

But when he did arrive, it turned out he had been at court for a long time looking for me. When I wasn't outside, he had parked, put in his quarter. And went inside. And went upstairs to all the judge's chambers to see if I was there.

And then he got my call on his cellphone.

I felt terrible that I had not been able to reach him in time.

He was sitting in my backyard in the sunshine petting my cat Priscilla who was in ecstasy at all his loving wonderful pets and rubs.

I told him my whole story from beginning to end.

He wasn't interested in my story except for what happened about the appointment with seeing the judge.

All he said when I finished my story was "well at least you got home."

I said "Jim I discovered I love taking the bus. I wished I could take the bus everywhere. So now we know when I have to go to court to see the judge, you can take me there.

But when it is over I can cross the street to the bus terminal and take bus home

"You don't have to pick me up."

I had gotten out all my magic markers after he called, and decided when he arrives I will have him draw a tattoo on my back.

I have been dying for a tattoo for 20 years. Watching the guy on the bus draw a tattoo on back of his hand with magic markers gave me good idea.

I showed Jim the magic markers and said "Make a flower. It doesn't have to be good because when I get out of the pool it will be gone."

So he drew a flower on my back with my magic markers. He did it in 4 seconds!

I wasn't going to go swimming, I thought I had enough adventures for one day.

When I was lying in the sunshine waiting for Jim to come, my Higher Self said, "You had a great experience." She said, "A great experience means tears and laughter and all new experiences."

I was surprised She called it a great experience, because some of it was bad, but I let Her talk me into it.

Jim said he has to go back to his club anyway because he

left his swim bag there. So I said "OK I may as well take my swim."

It was so nice arriving and seeing the familiar and wonderful girls behind the desk, and then going in the pool and wonderful Nancy and sweet lifeguard. And I told them the whole story and showed them my tattoo.

I said "I hope it is a flower but you never know what someone does behind your back," and I burst out laughing.

They said "it is a pretty flower."

I only got to swim a little because I arrived so late and was chatting with Nancy and lifeguard. But the last 5 minutes was great and the hot shower was great.

I said to Nancy "I have to be lickety-split because Jim is coming at noon and after what I put him thru this morning I don't want to make him wait."

And Jim was there when I got out and we had fun in the car.

I told him "I showed everyone your tattoo and they loved it."

And he looked and said, "There is nothing there now. After all my hard work."

I said "Next time draw a scary rattlesnake and we'll take picture of it.

"I'll send the pic to my friends on email, they won't know it is magic markers.

"I will say 'here I am with my new tattoo.'"

He got into it. He said "I'll draw one with fangs and blood dripping from his fangs."

"Fine!" I said, "I will tell my friends the best tattoo artist in Tucson did it."

And he laughed at being called a tattoo artist.

So I guess all's well that ends well.

I sure was happy girl when he dropped me off and headed right back to my sunshine with my ice cold orange soda.

After court I swim with my new tattoo

May 2nd

I Go Before the Judge

Back in court for another go at it

It was odd interesting intense crazy and something I don't want to do again.

I didn't spend the week before rehearsing what I was going to say to the judge because I had already done that back in February when the date on the summons said show up in court on February 28th.

I thought I was going to go before the judge then. And for weeks before, I went thru scenarios in my mind of what I would say to the judge.

But when I showed up at traffic court at 8 AM the clerk said "Do you want to pay your fines now, go to traffic school or have a hearing?"

I said "I want a hearing."

So she said "Go home and you will get in the mail the date set for your hearing. It will arrive within 2 weeks."

And sure enough 2 weeks later the letter arrived in the mail saying my hearing was set for April 30th at 2:30 PM.

Since it was almost 2 months away I put it out of my mind. Memorized the date, April 30th, and tacked it up on my bulletin board.

I didn't bring it back into my mind till April was well advanced. The week before I looked on my calendar and saw that it was a Tuesday.

And that morning when Jim was driving me to the pool I said "A week from today is my day in court. It's in the afternoon so we can swim in the morning and you can take me to court in the afternoon."

And from that moment on I was aware of going to court the following week.

But I didn't go back to rehearsing what I was going to say. Instead I just thought about logistics.

I thought Jim doesn't have to sit with me all thru it, he can go swim at his club and pick me up when it's over. I just have to bring quarters for the public telephone and tell him to pick up his messages in case he is swimming when his phone rings.

When the weekend before it arrived, I did start to go to it in my mind, and start saying in my mind what I will say to the judge.

But I really didn't want to do that again. So instead I connected to Judge John in my mind, let him love me. And he said I don't have to do that, he will tell me what to say at the time.

So every time my mind went back to it, I nipped it in the bud, and switched over to just letting him love me.

And the evening before my Higher Self said to me, "Anne the outcome doesn't matter. Whether you have to pay the fine or not doesn't matter. It is a great opportunity for you to go there and send love to everyone. You can bless the court by sending love to everyone. That is all you have to do and that is all that matters."

So that relaxed me. After all sending love in my mind is my favorite thing to do anyway, and easy as pie, and I was relieved to find out the outcome didn't matter at all.

The young lady officer who had given me all that trouble, had a partner, a man who looked about 10 years older than her and a lot more experienced.

He had been the one who handed me the two tickets. The first one because my learners permit had expired, "This is for driving without a license," he said.

And the second for driving in the bike lane.

And with it a tiny printed up pamphlet which explained about the tickets.

Which Jim immediately began to study.

He said "I can't find driving in bike lane on here, you have to look it up on your computer.

"But for expired license, they take the fine away if you show the judge you have a new license."

So the next morning he took me down to DMV so I could take my written test again and get a new learners permit.

I hadn't expected I would have to take that test again, Jim kept insisting "they will just extend it for you."

But he was wrong, I did have to take it again.

So on the spot I took it again.

I was allowed 6 wrong answers, but I got 7 wrong answers so I flunked.

Jim got a new copy of the drivers manual for me and as soon as I got home I read it from beginning to end.

The next morning we went back and I took it again. It was totally suspenseful for me. After 6 wrong answers I knew I couldn't get another one.

But instead of praying I got it right, I just prayed that I wouldn't cry if I got it wrong. "Big deal!" I said to myself, "all it would mean is I have to come back tomorrow and take it again."

Of course I really didn't want to, but neither was I going to ruin my happiness over it.

But by a miracle and all my guesses I did pass. I was elated and Jim took me swimming.

I had my new learners permit and could show it to the judge so that ticket would be taken away.

A week or 2 later when it was so cold and dreary being in the swim pool and Jim wasn't coming for another 1/2 hour I sat in the waiting room of the Y going thru my purse.

This is before I went to court the first time.

I found my two tickets at the bottom of my purse and the little pamphlet with them the man officer had given me. And looked up both my violations in the pamphlet.

For driving without a license it said $70. But if you show the judge you have a valid license the judge will take away your fine.

I could not find driving in the bike lane on it.

Jim told me to look it up on the computer because he hadn't found it there either. But I couldn't find it on the computer either.

When I went to court the first time, the clerk said do I want to pay the tickets, go to traffic school or have a hearing.

"How much are both tickets together?" I asked. I thought if driving without a license is only $70 probably driving in the bike lane will be $35.

But she said "both come to $340."

So I said "I want a hearing."

I did the arithmetic after I left her and realized they were going to charge me $270 for the bike lane.

I wanted to show her my new learners permit, but she said "show it to the judge."

My Afternoon in Court

Jim dropped me off in front of the court house a little before 1:30 and my Higher Self said "tell him to pick you up at 3:15."

Jim said fine, he will meet me right here where he dropped me off.

"Fine," I said.

I wanted to get there an hour before my case was called so I could get my bearings and be familiar with everything before my own case.

I found going thru the metal detector and being wanded lots of fun. To me it is like a game. And the guard told me, "Look on the door outside Information to find out where to go."

There was my name, but to my shock it said Judge Karen Smith. I wondered who Judge John was that I had been sharing so much love with in my mind. I felt like I had to start from scratch now.

It said Second Floor Courtroom 9. So I walked up the steps and found Court Room 9. It seemed like a sleepy almost empty room.

There was the girl judge up in front. She had blond hair

and looked like a nice woman. The law clerk next to her. And less than a handful of people sitting there.

I was very early and sat at the edge of one bench near the door. And began sending love in my mind to the judge and to everyone there. The clock did not seem to move at all.

Finally she called the first case. A cop sat down on one side, a young man on the other side. The cop said he did not obey the sign. The young man said the sign could not be seen. It had happened at night and he showed pictures to the judge to prove the sign could not be seen.

The judge said "I am going to take these pictures with me and study it for consideration. You will hear tomorrow."

Next came a cop with a lady. He said she had driven thru a stop sign. She said "I was not driving, it was my friend who was driving."

She actually proved this to the judge, and she dismissed her case.

Then the judge said to me "Your Officer is a little late. We are waiting for him."

So I knew the cop was coming and my case would not be dismissed because no cop showed up. Which is what I had secretly hoped for.

So then the judge left by a door next to the bench. And all that was left in the room was a couple sitting together and the law clerk. And I went back to sending love to the judge and to everyone.

The clock did not seem to move altho two cops arrived and sat in the special area for cops.

I went back to sending love and wondered if that clock would ever move. I looked around and was surprised to see art all over the walls. Framed paintings.

The judge did not reappear. I tried to focus on sending love but it was still almost 2 hours before Jim was supposed to pick me up. I was sure I would get out so early and wondered about a long time waiting for him.

I went back to sending love in my mind to the judge and to everyone in the court room, but it all felt so quiet and sleepy that my eyes started to close over.

I caught myself and began to focus on sending love again when suddenly I jerked fully awake. My own cop had appeared.

I had assumed the man cop her partner would be the one, but it was HER! I hadn't realized I hated her till I saw her again for the first time in court. She had been very mean to me in every possible way.

She looked so tall, with such long legs, and without her cap, had very pretty chestnut wavy hair down to her collar.

And she looked nervous. Not like all the other cops. And was in a light grey uniform, not in their dark blue one, and did not look heavily armed as they did. But maybe I didn't see her gun.

As soon as she arrived my praying began in earnest. I now had a real purpose for sending love, I wanted to take away the hate in my mind.

I moved over on the bench so a pillar obstructed my view of her, and her view of me. And I just focused on sending love to her. I did that for quite a while till I was completely harmonious with her in my mind. And then I sent love to her and the judge.

And to my surprise I heard her let out a little cough. She did it two times. I knew what that cough meant. Her mind was responding to all that love.

I was surprised that she was the only one who responded to all the love I had been steadily sending out since I arrived. The judge, the clerk, the cops, the other people who had been waiting for their cases, the couple who still was— no one had responded. Only Officer

Jeffries, my arresting officer, responded.

I realized she must be a sensitive girl.

Finally the judge returned. And called my case. We both stood up and raised our right hand and swore to tell the truth, the whole truth and nothing but the truth. Which I fully intended to do and which I did.

Officer Jeffries spoke first. She identified herself. And said she has been on the force since December 2012.

So she had been a cop for just weeks when she stopped me. That explained why she had done such a botched job in every way. She had no experience and no natural talent for the job to boot.

And she is so young, she looked around 23 or 24 the most.

Officer Jeffries testified to the judge that I had been driving nearly a mile in the bike lane and when she stopped me the first thing she asked me was "why was I driving in the bike lane?" And that I had answered "I feel safe driving in the bike lane."

All of this is hooey and never happened.

As I told the judge when it was my turn to talk, "I am learning how to drive. I am now expert at driving around my own residential neighborhood but am just learning how to drive in traffic.

"I had decided to drive to the mini Post Office which is in the residential neighborhood across Speedway Boulevard.

"I waited till there was no traffic coming in the opposite direction, signaled that I was going to turn, but when I looked in my mirror cars were bearing down on me.

"This kept happening, so finally I signaled right, changed lanes and pulled into the bike lane, first looking to see there were no bikes. So I could stop and figure out what I was going to do. All I wanted was to get out of everyone's way.

"However the instant I pulled into the bike lane my friend said 'there is a cop behind you.' I looked in the mirror and sure enough there was.

"I thought the cops would stop me, but instead they kept following me in the bike lane. I had no idea why the cops wanted me to keep driving in the bike lane. Finally they signaled that I should pull over into a driveway behind a building and I did.

"She never asked me why I was in the bike lane. All she said to me is 'license and registration please.' She discovered my learners permit had expired.

"Then I had to sit there for a very long time. And then the man cop got out and gave me two tickets, one for driving in the bike lane, and one for expired license.

"I went down the next day and took the written test all over again and got a new learners permit. Here is my new learners permit. Do you want to see it?"

"No I don't!" the Judge said, "You can show it to the officer if you like."

I was so surprised.

Jim had told me 100 times to make sure I have my new license with me to show the judge so I would not have to pay that fine. As if I would have forgotten to bring it!

So Officer Jeffries obediently held out her hand to see my new learners permit. Looked at it and handed it back to me. It made no sense to me.

Then the judge asked her about my testimony. And Officer Jeffries said "What she said is exactly what happened."

I was gratified.

So then the judge said I had to pay $195 the fine for driving in the bike lane because I was driving in the bike lane. I said "OK."

Then she said I have to pay the fine for driving without

a valid license.

"When do you think you will get your drivers license?" she said to me.

I thought and said "Maybe around same time the monsoons come." (In Tucson that is July 4th.)

She said, "You can come back then and show it to me and you won't have to pay the fine."

I said "Maybe I will just pay the $70 and get it over with. I'll pay both fines now. All I want is to learn how to drive. I don't want to come to court again. How much do both fines come to?"

She said "Driving in the bike lane is 195 and driving without a license is 205."

I said "But I got my new learners permit. I got it the day afterwards."

At that point the judge got very sympathetic but also thought I was a total idiot. She tried every which way to Sunday to explain to me that I needed a drivers license to drive.

I kept trying to say the pamphlet the officer gave me said 70 dollars and I went down the next day and I have my new learners permit.

When she tried to say again I need a drivers license to

drive, I interrupted her. I said "I know I need a drivers license to drive. I am not stupid!"

I didn't even try again to find out why it was 205 instead of 70 like the pamphlet said.

By now she was totally sympathetic and on my side just thought she was dealing with a jerk.

She said "I understand you are learning how to drive, maybe you should go to a professional driving school rather than have your friend teach you.

"I'll tell you what I'll do. I'll give you till August 30th to get your license. And if you need more time just call me."

She was such a darling and trying to be so sweet to me. I wanted to say "I love you." Instead I just mouthed the words. I didn't think you were allowed to say "I love you" out loud to a judge at court.

So I went to the clerk so he could do the paperwork for me. He had everything that was especially pertinent blocked out in yellow.

He too like the rest of the court room— Judge Karen, Officer Jeffries, the policemen waiting in the box. And the people who had arrived while my case was going on— all thought I was the biggest idiot in the western world.

But I didn't care. I knew in my heart of hearts it was

good for me to have a deadline to get my real drivers license. And the deadline the judge had given me was a good deadline. I actually was in a great mood and loved everyone.

I thought it was a great outcome. I even teased Officer Jeffries as she was standing up in the witness box. "Stay out of my neighborhood!" I said to her. "Stay away from me! If you see me, pretend you don't!"

And I giggled and went down to pay my fine.

I was surprised to see that it was ten after 3. I guess my case had taken a long time.

I was completely merry and happy. It was all over and I thought it was a good outcome. The law clerk had told me to go to the Information Room downstairs to pay my fine

I asked the girl at the desk "how do I pay my fine?" She gave me a number and said, "it will take one minute for you to be called."

And sure enough after one minute, I was called to Window 17.

I got out my credit card and paid the 195 for driving in the bike lane. And then I giggled to the girl about how I have till August 30th to get my regular license.

I showed her that paper work. I said how the judge said

call her if I want more time.

"What is her phone number?"

She said "We don't have it, you'd have to come down here for that."

"It's not worth it to me," I said. "It's more better for me to get my license by August 30th. Can I just show it to you or will I have to show it to the judge?" She said I can show it to her.

I believed her and thought, well then everything is perfect. "Great!" I said.

I was laughing the whole time. I have no idea why I was in such an up mood.

I looked at the clock and it was 3:15 on the dot. I walked out and there was a hot dog man right there. Sitting in one hard chair in the shade with another chair right next to him.

Jim was not there. I was so thirsty and just wanted a cigarette. "Do you have sodas?" I asked.

"Yes," he said.

"What soda do you want?"

He opened up his cooler, all the cans of sodas on ice.

"I wanted a Coke, that seemed perfect after a whole day in court, but I see you have Pepsi. That is fine."

"I have a Coke," he said.

And handed it to me.

"How much?" I said.

"One dollar," he said.

I got out 2 dollar bills. I handed him one for the soda, and another one saying "After a day in court I want luck. This is for you." He was happy to get it.

I looked at the chair right next to him in the shade. "Can I sit here and smoke a cigarette while waiting for my friend to pick me up?"

"Of course," he said.

He was such a nice short Mexican man. Just who you want to see after your afternoon in court.

I was just about to sit comfortably down next to this lovely man, with my soda in my hand and my cigarettes in my purse when Jim drove up.

I got in the car with my unopened can of Coke and sat next to him.

"Well you missed a great show," I said to him. "They all think I am a total idiot. I finally had to tell the judge I'm not stupid and I told Officer Jeffries to stay out of my neighborhood. And I have to get my drivers license by August 30th or pay $205.

"OK" Jim said, "we'll start practicing your tushy turns

tomorrow."

"OK" I said.

It took me forever to calm down from my experience.

Altho my Higher Self said, "You did spectacular Anne.
You gave love to everyone plus you gave them all a great
show."

But when I woke up the next morning all I could think
was "How could I have made such an idiot of myself in
court!"

Jim has fantasies about Officer Jeffries. He likes girls with
long legs

Love, Annie

May 9th 2013
Tucson Arizona

All cartoons are by my husband, Bill Pyne

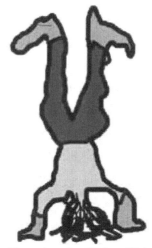

Drawing by Helen Kritzler
For Anne's new novel Topsy Turvy

Thank you for reading my little tale. They are a few chapters from my new novel, **Topsy Turvy** about my first 6 months in this totally unusual year 2013. I plan to publish it this summer.
 I love you
Annie

Muchas gracias to everyone in Tucson for being so swell to me. I am so grateful to have all you angels in my life…

And for my great angels who help me so much. Frank Grijalva and Bill Kraft. Better friends a girl could not have.

Haiku Helen Press

Books by Anne Wilensky

Novels

Ruthie Has a New Love

Girl Blog From Tucson

More Girl Blog From Tucson

Sweet Sound of Bird Song

Haboob

And my little women's lib book

Not What You'd Expect
How the women's liberation movement started
My personal experience of it

Haiku Helen Press is Anne Pyne and Helen Kritzler who met in the women's liberation movement in the Sixties and have been friends ever since.

Annie and Helen are Haiku Helen Press

Made in the USA
Charleston, SC
24 September 2015